AISHA

The story of the Northern Nigeria girl child, the perils and woes of insurgencies and terrorism

Moses Opara Chibueze

CHAPTER ONE

LEAVING HOME

It was a harmattan season, everywhere was dusty and cold as tension occupied the sky. Aisha woke up in the middle of the night to see her mother panting like someone whose heart would rip off the next minute. She had not had sufficient sleep for the past weeks. Her thoughts had been unstable, she always thought of her late husband who was killed in an ambush by the rebels. And her children Aisha and Abdullahi who were 10 and 7 years of age. She was afraid not to lose them to the cold hands of death. When a person is hurting, they often just want everyone to leave them alone. They build protective walls around themselves, not only to keep other people out but also to guard their hearts against unclear emotions... Six months after the burial of her husband. She still sees his image around her. She wakes every morning, quarterly unchained from the memories they shared, only to have memories walk in to break her heart with cruel faces of death. Her grieving heart could not allow her to sleep and her thoughts were blank all through the night. To her, an hour is like many days, and a year is like forever. She could not bear the pains of seeing herself as a widow and her children live every day without a father. Tears rushed down her eyes as she had lost a part of herself that can't be replaced. She was not herself again, she was always feeling like the world had left her, she was in between her dreams and waking life knitting her heart with fragments of silence every moment. "Mother, rest, please rest" Aisha's voice embraced the room. "the thoughts of your father remind me of me our fitting ends, the promises, I am now a widow among the missing," she replied, with a soft voice not her own...

You stand on the verge, seeing how life passes in front of you. You look at yourself all over again, only to find out the person you are had been dead for long, and you are just acting another person's script with a life that is not your own. You await your heart to reply only to hear voices telling you another version of yourself. That feeling of living yourself behind your unending nightmares, with various insomnia, and night walking.

You try to look for your heart but it is no longer where you left it... The cloud was filled with grief and sorrow, the village was quiet, and also it is the smallest among all other villages. The villagers were only left with their fearful voices to fend for themselves in the dark. Many of them were too afraid to wash their pants of urine. Many had anemia of doubt. The rebels had attacked a village close to theirs and had sent a letter to their village head that they would come for them next.

...

It was 3 am, they heard screams of gunshots and bombs far away. "Mother, have they come to send us to the dust," Aisha said with fear written all over her face. Abdul was still sleeping, curled like a hopeless child on a hopeless raffia mat on the floor. They have come to get us, Aisha, wake your brother let us run for safety. She went to knock at her widow friend's door, mama Jamil whose only child was killed by the rebels on his way to Maduguire to write his Jamb examination. She woke up confused and didn't know what to do. The gunshots were drawing nearer. The villagers had woken up from their misplaced dreams to find the nearest escape root to save their lives. Some ran into the dark forest while some were still confused about what to do. Aisha woke Abdul up and gave him worn-out clothing to put on his torn shorts. While she dressed up too. Her mother came in and took some items they would need on their way. They set out to escape through a thick forest.

....

The rebels came in covered robes chanting the name of their god. Some are very young and some old. They were happily shooting and destroying things.

The village was burnt down and nothing was spared. Some people were beheaded while others who couldn't escape were burnt alive. Before the military men could reach the village. The rebels had fled with the things they looted from the villagers. Aisha was clouded with thoughts too heavy for her mind. She held her mother's right hand while Abdullahi held her left hand and was walking with rented steps. Mama Jamil looked weak, she sat down panting hoping the forest will be in their favor.

Many thoughts rush through her mind. She imagined the rebels coming towards them, her home, and what is ahead of them. "they preach peace, but are against it. What kind of life is this?" mama Jamil said with sadness written all over her face.

...

The sun had started setting on the lips of the west. They had to run fast so that the night won't rest on their hearts. Abdullahi broke down and started crying. The cause of his tears no one knew. Aisha embraced him and brought out some pieces of leftover yam from her bag and gave it to him. It was obvious he was very hungry. Her mother, Ralia looked at him and a drop of tears fell from her eyes. Mama Jamil sat beside a barren tree looking at them, she also broke into tears and rained ungodly causes on the rebels in her dialect. "what are they fighting for? Why are they killing the innocent? Is it for a religious or political purpose of Allah sent them to kill the innocent ones? No, Allah is love and Islam is a religion of peace. I don't know where they got their doctrines and who told them Allah is evil and delights in their evil acts." she said to break the silence. Ralia could not say anything. She was busy consoling herself.

...

It was getting dark, they were lost in the forest. They only had with them prayers to guide them through. They encountered piles of dead bodies. Some died as a result of hunger and some were massacred. They were lucky that the rebels had divorced that path of the forest for another village. Aisha spoke with a calm voice. Kaka, as she always calls her mother, look over there. She looked and saw a few men in Khaki holding guns. They went closer to undress their fears and realized they were soldiers lying in ambush for the rebels. They approached them with joy and big sighs of relief. The soldiers gave them a warm welcome and some food to eat with a place for them to sleep for the night. They didn't want to be distracted from the ambush. Soldier Ponjul is the commander of the troop. He is a friendly and kind man. He always wore a big laugh on his face. He raised Abdullahi up and down and asked him if he would like to be a soldier. He didn't object to be a soldier and protect his family and country from the hands of the rebels. Abdullahi asked sergeant Ponjul a few questions while Aisha sat down observing the environment and was wondering how the soldiers stay up at night not minding their lives, but that of others. She broke the silence, Abdullahi had slept off. "soldier Ponjul, are you people paid well?" he laughed aloud to dodge the question. She continued, "you soldiers are giving your all," she said with a half-smile on her face. "Aisha, I like your intelligence. You have shown me that there is still hope for our country. You are a child with great understanding. I didn't take the job for the money, but the love of my country. Some took the job for the money, to be feared and accorded with respect as uniform men, but mine is to protect and guide my country from the hands of rebels and those who don't want peace to reign." he paused and wiped his face with a handkerchief.

Her eyes were filled with tears, she hugged him and smiled, and went to sleep.

...

The morning was fast to come. Sounds of birds were heard on the trees littered around the forest. All the soldiers woke up to prepare for another ambush. The rebels didn't follow that route last night they attacked another village but were unlucky to meet a battalion of readily equipped soldiers, who deprived them of their evil plans. Sergeant Keshi, one of the soldiers woke them up to prepare for the IDP camp in the heart of the city. Other soldiers mounted with faces filled with insufficient sleep. Aisha sat beside sergeant Ponjul in one of the vans. While Abdullahi was with his mother and Mama Jamil in another. He told her stories of the Fulani herdsmen in Jos and Benue states. He recounted how his friends Usman and Segun were killed during a bloody gunfight with the herdsmen on a Christmas eve, and how they killed people like chickens. "How do they get their guns?" Aisha asked with pity.

"They use sophisticated weapons while we use worn-out ones suffering from cold and mental kwashiorkor. We are not well equipped and provided for that is why it seems as if they are winning the battle. People don't know how much we dedicate our lives to protect their interests. I stopped reading the newspapers because they are filled with diluted truths. At times, they will report only five soldiers died, and they are taken care of, but we know the truth you all don't know. You only know what they want you to know. I know I will die one day. But if I die on the battleground, how will the country I gave my all celebrate my battalion and me? How will they care for my family and that of my battalions? I don't expect much from life again. It is filled with sorrow and joy. We live today and tomorrow we die, what is the meaning of life?

...

My mother told me that the rebels killed my father with some of his friends. Aisha looked away as tears clouded her eyes. "Little Aisha, you will grow up to become a woman one day. Your education is very important, don't allow anyone to take it away from you. You and your family will be fine at the IDP camp. Just make sure you take good care of your mother and brother. We shall see again maybe in heaven." Sergent Ponjul said with a calm voice and embraced her. The van halted at the IDP camp. Some young soldiers guiding the camp stood at attention as Sergent Ponjul alighted. He released them and had a chit chat with them. He would be living soon with his troops for another location in the Sambisa forest. There were many people there, some were half-mad, confused, sorrowful, joyful, and lost. The camp was filled with mixed emotions. Ralia and mama Jamil were a bit relieved. They were taken to one of the tents in the camp, it was tattered, dirty, and filled with starvation. Ralia asked one of the women how they feed and have their bathe. She replied, with a mock smile. We eat twice a day and if you don't go early you will starve all day. For bathing, we struggle. It is survival for the fittest.

Aisha sat beside a small boy who looked sick and unhealthy as a result of malnutrition. She missed home and its warmth. The love her family shared before the insurgence. She thought of what Sergeant Ponjul told her, not to allow anything to take away her education. She smiled and prayed for him hoping one day she will make him proud. She brought out a pen and a torn book from her bag to write down her experience in the forest and how they survived the attack of the rebels. She looked at her mother and brother walking with some women to get their dinner. She sighed and smiled. She thought of the rebels and why they derived joy in killing people.

"If they uphold religion and tribe with zeal

Let them also uphold lives

For where love and peace are lost

Religion and tribe are only but walking corpses"

She wrote down these lines and smiled at the sick little small boy looking at her with seriousness. She was left with her dreams and hope to fend for themselves. She knew tomorrow will be better and nothing will take away her education. She walked slowly, to catch up with her mother and brother. The cloud was filled with groaning and horror. Every day brings its fears and hope. Love does not end with death, it remains in the heart.

CHAPTER 2

A STRING OF HOPE

Aisha was awake, she couldn't find sleep. Everywhere was dark and nude. She was afraid the rebels would attack them again. She was afraid her nightmare would come into reality. She sat on a one-legged stool beside the door, side by side with her unfiltered dreams only to discover her mind had wandered away from her. Her mother and brother were fast asleep. She stood up and left the room that occupied over 20 people. Some slept like a log, others were with their burdens by their side. Others had done away with their pains and were comfortable they were safe. She stood up from the stool and went outside to feel the warmth of the night. Everywhere looked like a ghost land, the night watchmen were walking up and down to make sure they were all safe. She overheard one of them saying there was a bomb blast not far from the IDP camp and ten people died and some girls were kidnapped from their school in one of the local government areas by the rebels. Her heart was full of fear nowhere was safe in the state. Death and fear we're not far away. Parents were afraid to lose their children, children were afraid to lose their parents, and afraid of school, because they may get killed or kidnapped.

The camp was filled with dreams. Children, young and old. Living with the picture of their dreams. Many of them want to be educated, some want to revenge the death of their parents like Abdullahi who wanted to be a soldier, some had dreams that were not too big to dream. At times death comes to them unannounced. They suffer poor medical care and the food they eat suffers from malnutrition. Some have terminal diseases, kwashiorkor, marasmus, malaria, typhoid were constant visitors. Some of them are almajiris, who had lost their paths but held survival on their neck. The government at times overlooked them until elections are drawing nearer. There was too much hypocrisy in our country, hidden in kindness.

Aisha walked towards one of the security men who was flashing his torch towards her. He looked like someone above 40 and above. He was also a victim of the insurgence. He had a very big business in his village not until the rebels came and stole everything and killed his children and wife before he could return from Maiduguri where he went to buy goods for his shop. The news of their death broke his heart and put him in the situation he is in. Since then he came to believe that Allah gives and Allah takes. He flashed his torch again towards Aisha who was coming towards him.

"Kai, manene?" he screamed in his dialect. "Good evening sir, it is your daughter" Aisha replied.

She sat closer to him and gave him a smile that had in it a flash of hope. He could not send her back nor scold her any further.

"baba, I just came with my family three days ago. The rebels chased us away from our home and when we narrowly escaped, we ran without taking our belongings we only left with our fears." She said,

Baba laughed, held her hand, and smiled.

"Violence and conflict had swallowed the state since 2009. My wife and children were killed in cold nakedness. I have been here since 2013 and here is my second home. If one is not careful here one will realize one is every day leaving oneself and spirit inside one.

"Baba, how have you been surviving the fear of every day"? Her voice pierced through his heart.

"Some NGOs come at times to share relief materials to us, some come with foodstuff, clothes, shoes, and toiletries. It had been easy for some of us that are old and trying to survive. At times, when. They refuse to walk our path, we find every means to survive." he said, as his eyes were filled with strange tears he could not hold. Like a wilderness of silence, a fear deep within him listened and waited.

"Baba, we shall overcome. Hope is all we need after this storm," she said and stood to leave...

Weak tears rose to her eyes, of gladness, for the nebulous safety, she had come to, of pains, for the famished and divorced roads that had brought her to the camp. The darkness began to frown, a frown accompanied by silence. The camp oozed of many lost dreams, drowning fears, clouded shame, and dark hopes. The camp was filled with many untold stories buried in their minds. She walked slowly in the dark with her hope as if the darkness was waiting for her. She wore a nameless smile as situations peeped into her soul. There was a change in the quality of her silence. Silence in her like the grave. She was left all alone. She was left with her fate. She just needed a hand to hold her. An embrace that will tell her to remain strong...

CHAPTER 3

EVERY DAY BRINGS ITS FEAR

Aisha woke up at the sound of a bird chirping on a barren tree close to the weeping tent. The IDP camp was like a lost town, everyone was nursing two or more pains. It was filled with ghosts of painful memories carrying the horrors of the past along with them. She tried to wake her mother and brother who were still asleep and left to feel the warmth of the morning but left them to themselves. She went straight to baba who was listening to the morning news. His body was distant and half with him. She sat beside him in the silence only the radio was whispering the voice of the newscaster...

"Somewhere in Barkin-Ladi, 1.4 million people were displaced by some gunmen that posed as Fulani herdsmen!" the newscaster's voice was soft and calm over the radio. Some said they were rebels. Some said they were sent by some politicians who want to destroy the government. Different news with mixed lies filled the air. The truth was far from everyone. Baba said, with a half-smile. He narrated a story of the rebels attacks "In Dapachi North-Eastern city of Borno, to Aisha who was looking keenly at him while listening to the newscaster.

One fateful morning. "They announced their arrival by shooting in the air and gathered some men both young and old and killed them. Some fled to Chad, Niger, and Cameroon, but others remained to die with their dreams. Some lost themselves and their children while trying to escape death. The ones that couldn't flee from their shadows were shot dead by the rebels who spoke in a strange language. They made sure they took the soul of the village with them and raped both old and young women repeatedly. They took many of them along with them and killed others that proved stubborn. Some were married off and molested every night until the military men came to save them from their nightmares and the cruelty of the rebels who turned them to war botties. Death has turned our homes to its own." baba said as he turned to another station.

"Every day brings its fear." She said. And silence embraced the moment. Everyday violence wore another look. The IDP camp keeps increasing in the number of people fighting for scanty spaces, survival as they are counting their days. The camp was filled with malnourished children, many of them living with the memories of their dead or absent parents who eloped leaving their responsibilities behind. They jumped around, seeking attention, reaching out for hands to give them hope with dreams written in their souls. The newborn babies arrive with death written on their foreheads, they arrive to see death like a neighbor and believe it will have its moment one day. Some were strangers to themselves. They sleep and wake up with half expectations...

CHAPTER 4

THE SMELL OF FEAR

A righteous smell of fear clouded the camp. As the camp children were living their daily reality. Hungry, bored, looking sick and a quarter to go, like a lost generation. They don't only suffer the fear and horrors they try to do away from their hearts, but the holy hypocrisy of the government that posed as their messiah but mocked them behind. Aisha could see death written in her brother's eyes who was suffering from an unnamed sickness. She could see pains written all over her mother who prayed day and night for her son not to die. The pain of every mother hoping death hisses at them and not their children.

The camp was diagnosed with a disease of fear. Every day children died of diarrhea and cholera. Their mothers looked faintly at them with mixed tears. At times, you wonder how they sleep in the tent, covered with a tattered tarpaulin that exposed their predicaments and the privacy they try to keep. You wonder how mothers sleep at night, with so many children with the smell of fear and death around them. You wonder how they survive during the rainy season and the flooding it comes with. The rashness of the harmattan that pieces through the bones. The foul smell from the naked toilets and bathrooms was accompanied by horrible flies and mosquitoes that mocked them. The cold that embraced their fears and the smell of depression unknown.

At times when the rain comes, they have no place to sit, no place to spread down their dreams, no place to consult their heads, no place to call home. They become imprisoned by the rains and pray night and day for the rain to disappear. Every night, when it rains, they hang on the air and nod away from the remaining sleep that wants to nurture... What is life when everything is taking away from you and you are left to survive the harshness of life accompanied by phases of survival? What will you do when life doesn't keep its promises but stones you with pebbles of hardship you didn't bargain for that will want you to subscribe to suicide? Every day in the

IDP we are in a constant battle between the living and dying.

The sky was low and nearly dark and the air too cruel to breathe. Aisha looked at her mother with an impatient frown. She looked old, black, and patient, smelling of poverty, sickness, and death. "Kaka, as she calls her why are you sad?"' she asked. Her mother took long before she answered. She looked like a stranger within her. She missed her husband, her home, her joy, and the presence of her family. "Aisha, she spoke in her dialect. There is hope. One day we shall return home if death says no to us." she said as tears flooded her eyes. Abdullahi sat on a stunted branch of a tree closer to their tent looking sickly at other children playing a tattered football. Aisha stood up and left her mother to meet him, she could only see the energy of survival in his eyes and his smile that weaved her emotions. She held his hands as they watched the children together with laughter too strong to chase their doubts. Too strong to parch their fates and too strong to encourage them.

Chapter 5

SITUATIONS CREATE THERE OWN SOLUTIONS

Some people deeply feel for others whether it's their joy or sorrow. They become a part of their emotions, part of their existence, and part of their fears. They go about with wondering hopes, believing pain and pleasure are parts of life. An air of wretchedness and misery strolled through the camp. It was air-filled with groaning. The journey of life is not an easy one. There are times your life makes you kneel on the ground and you feel that it is over. You feel useless. You start questioning your worth. Your existence and all.

...

Aisha sat alone in her company looking at her mother from a dwarf distance who was lost in thoughts while Abdullahi slept on a hopeless raffia mat beside her.

"Aisha, what are you doing here this hour of the day"? A soft voice shook her fears. It was Rebecca, an orphan, and one of the camp girls who was brought along with some 200 IDP's in a military van three months ago. She is of average height, dark, with a pointed nose and she always wore a sweet smile that reflects the state of her mind. They both knew each other when some NGOs came to give them hope.

"Rebecca, she gave her a half-smile and said nothing" she felt there was nothing to say. She felt every situation will create their solutions. Rebecca held her hands and saw the fears in her. She tried to call them by their names, but Aisha had worn them on her like a robe. Sherries to share some pages of her story and leave others to fend for themselves, but Aisha was not yet ready to listen.

Rebecca had the same vision as Aisha. She knew the importance of education and had vowed that no one would take it away from her. Her parents before they were murdered by the rebels will always tell her not to allow any situation to stop her from her education.

"Aisha" her call shook away her fear. This time she became lively.

"Rebecca, I am sorry for my reply earlier. Just that life has been cruel to me. I want to go to school. I want a real education. The school in this camp can't sharpen my mind. We learn in distress in a surrounding filled with filths. At times the smell strolls through our nose and occupy our minds" She looked away to avoid looking into her eyes. Rebecca was silent for a few minutes.

"The world that exists inside you, is the world you create outside you. Your education is you, don't trade it for anything." Rebecca embraced her. They were silent for a while. The sky above them looked was half clouded. It was the rainy season. They know if it rains they will do a vigil. They know the rain won't care for them. They stood up, held each other's hand, and walked down through the naked dreams of the field.

Chapter 6

IF TOMORROW COMES

The cloud yawned at midnight, everywhere was dark. They were afraid the rain has come and nothing they would do about it. Aisha woke up and tapped Rebecca who folded herself in a corner of the flat mattress. No sooner have they realized than the rain began. Everyone woke up to save their heads from the rain. Some nursing mothers backed their children to save them from the cold and the temporal flooding. The last rain was not kind to them, it brought several diseases, whooping cough, malaria, typhoid, and took away many of their scanty properties.

No one could sleep until the rain stopped. The tent was flooded with water, and they were left to scoop the water with a small rubber into a bucket to dispose of outside. Some kept the water so it will dissolve for them to use to bathe, wash their clothes, and drink. Tears are stories, at loss for words. Their homes were waiting for them where they left them, hoping they keep their promises and return. At times, they see fear and death as their life because, in reality, that's their life, they separate their experiences into two but later realize it is only one experience. One life. One death. Many fears and become grateful for the experience of living. Aisha and Rebecca stood in a corner with Abdullahi as the women including her mother tried to put the half-alive tent in order. Baba had left his tent to check on them, he was lucky his tent was not located at the flooding area of the camp. Aisha saw him and ran to him as Rebecca and Abdul followed suit like sheep.

"Baba," she said with tears in her eyes. She could no longer contain the pains she had been feeling since she arrived at the camp. The pain that she will lose her mother and Abdul. The pain that accompanied her to the camp.

"If life can bring you to the most unexpected situations. No matter how ready you are, not everything will go as you planned. Aisha, zai yi kyau." Baba said and left them outside to greet the women in the tent. He had been the voice of many of the IDP's in the camp. He teaches Aisha and Rebecca and some other young girls and boys who were eager for education arithmetic and the English language in his free time. Hoping one day they will leave the camp for a better place where they will have access to education.

It was a bright morning. Everywhere was wet. The birds sang on a distant tree and voices were littered everywhere. Some voices were after their children, some to awaken their sleeping bodies, some were of children welcoming the morning with tears. A piece of news was going round that some people in charge of the camp were stealing and reselling, the government and some kind-hearted NGOs brought for them. It was not quite long that the news was buried. The camp dwellers only murmured and frowned to show the displeasures of their worsening conditions and mental insecurities like people in need of a spiritual rehab. "Just yesterday, Foluke, Amina, and Ngozi were raped by some miscreants in the camp and no one cared to look into it. who cared to call the culprits out? Is this life we are living in? At times, we forget we are living" Aisha's mother said with an unbearable frown tormenting her smiles, as she tried to console one of the women whose child was suffering from acute typhoid.

Tomorrow was too far to come. They were left with the horrors no one could see. No one could feel. No one could touch. Only them with their thoughts looking at tomorrow and hoping if it will come.

CHAPTER 7

ANOTHER SIDE OF FEAR

Rebecca sat on a small piece of stone as the evening sun rested on her face. She was deep in thought. Her mind was occupied with the death of her parents in Gwoza. How she saw them from a distance being shot by the rebels. A burden of depression fell on her. A depression that at times flashes through the minds of many orphans. A depression that only faith could heal.

"I would have died along with my parents with dignity and rest than to live a life full of horror in this camp." She murmured. A soft hand parted her at the back, it was Daniel. One of the camp boys whose parents and five siblings were killed by the rebels. He was the only one who escaped through a narrow path that was not known by the rebels.

"My name is Daniel. I am your neighbor. How are you?" He gave her a believable smile that he won't hot her nor make her feel the heavens had forsaken her. She held her breath for a while and looked at him again as he sat beside her.

"My name is Rebecca, I am also your neighbor. " she reciprocated the smile and returned to her leftover thoughts.

Daniel looked like a young boy of 22 years old. He is dark and of average height, with pink lips and a pointed nose. His hair is well combed and his smile shows off his gap teeth and jovial nature. On his shirt was boldly written, "Be human, defend the undefended and help the helpless." He was able to put Rebecca back to herself. They both laughed and discussed different issues. Their families before their death, their education, the rebels, their homes, their difficulties, their tents in the camp, the hardship, and the hope.

"Rebecca' he called her name. "Yes, Daniel" she replied and looked at him.

"Be optimistic and true to yourself. Once you uplift your inner being, you will come to realize that life comes in black and white and that will make us grateful in every moment of our lives," he said with a spark of emotion on his face. She sighed a heavy sigh and looked up. Tears had started clouding her eyes. Daniel held her right hand. "We were forced to become orphans, we didn't plan it. We must not allow the pains that came here with us to take us out of the dreams we carry. There is no conflict here, be happy even if it is for a moment. Aisha is looking up to you because I always see you both together. We can't take the pains away and we can't let them kill us." He said as silence embraced the moment. Rebecca was still sobbing. She was playing Daniel's words over and over again in her mind. Daniel stood up with a smile on his face and left to join other camp boys in the field closer to the baba's tent. Rebecca's face was facing down, she was trading something on the ground with a small stick. "I will not trade my education for anything. Nothing will stop me from my education." She stood up with a scanty gaze and saw Aisha with baba sitting under a Melina tree with laughter all over their faces. The sky was gathering. "It seems it would rain again." She muttered and walked slowly dragging her feet towards Aisha's direction.

CHAPTER 8

FRAGILE EXISTENCE

A mysterious air of death enveloped the camp. Many wore sad faces waiting for their own time to die. A child in the camp had been convulsing and his mother was confused. She ran for help but help was nowhere. The women tried to assist the young boy but couldn't. He died before she returned. She wept and called the names of Allah! to help her. Other camp dwellers wept with her as she poured her emotions, liver her child, and dropped him on the ground. A woman who was at the point of given birth also died that morning. Aisha and Rebecca ran to call Baba. He came along with a gravedigger. They wrapped them with some pieces of clothing and took their bodies away to be buried. The corpse was accompanied by tears. Mama Kabiru is the name of the woman that died in labor. She was known all over the camp as a kind, caring, loving, and patient woman. Her son Kabiru died two days after they arrived at the camp. How she got pregnant is what we still find difficult to understand, because her husband was killed by the rebels. They were crying not that they had not seen death that is more than mama Kabiru's death but for the fact that they will miss her loving presence.

"Why do good people die?" Rebecca asked baba.

"We can't question Allah. He gives and takes. He knows our end from our beginning."

Some young men and women always stay under a huge tree a bit far from the camp to smoke wee wee to remove their minds from the horrors in the camp and the strange dreams that didn't want to go. At times, they wake up with hungry heads, tired minds, suicide, depression, and doubting their fragile existence. Aisha and Rebecca were working back to their tents in the evening, the weather was cold, windy, and cloudy they approached two young boys beside a bush at the camp smoking wee-wee. Abdul and Ishaku are friends from Dikwa. Abdul is dark and huge, one of his eyes looks dim and one of his hands is bent. He said his fleeing from the rebels brought the predicaments upon him. He talks with a deep voice that can scare anyone and looks fierce whenever he is angry. Ishaku is fair, slim, and tall. He has a cut on his head, he said he got it when he was trying to flee from the village when the rebels attacked. He is calm and easy going and a clear antonym of Abdul.

They were one of those whose houses were destroyed in the sudden attack by the rebels at Dikwa local government. They had three wraps of wee and some sachets of tramadol. Aisha greeted them "Sannu," she said. Ishaku replied but Abdul was lost within. She looked at them, but Rebecca wasn't interested because there had been news about rape in the camp. Aisha felt pity for them and tried to talk to them about education. Abdul stood up and left but Ishaku was interested.

"Why do you smoke wee-wee," Aisha asked him. Rebecca stood looking at him and also at Abdul walking towards an unknown direction.

"It makes us hard and takes away our pains. When the fear comes wee takes it away."

She spoke at length about the harmful effects of hair drugs and how it makes one do what Allah has called haram. She smiled at him after her lecture. He dropped the wee on him and promised her he would change and focus on his dreams... There was thunder in the sky. Ishaku headed towards Abdul while Aisha and Rebecca ran to the tent to prepare for the coming rain.

CHAPTER 9

WHAT WE ARE FIGHTING IS DEADLIER THAN FEAR

Aisha and Rebecca sat beside baba to listen to the evening news on BBC. A rumor was carried that morning some soldiers were ambushed at Baga and 40 of them died. Aisha remembered Sergent Ponjul and Keshi said they would fight from Baga. She prayed in her heart that nothing bad should happen to them. Her thoughts were restless, she adjusted herself to listen to the news. The broadcaster confirmed the news about the killings. "some soldiers were ambushed at Baga and forty died." She said in an accent that is not her own.

Baba shook his head and looked at the girls. I want to tell both of you about my soldier friends and what they told me the last day I saw them before they left for Gashiga where they were killed in an ambush. "can a man fight on an empty stomach"? He asked them. They chorused no.

"At times, you wonder if those sending roses soldiers into the bush to fight are righteous and not corrupt. Do you wonder where they sleep and how they feed? And many thoughts pass through your mind." baba said and clears his throat to tell them about his friends. An air of silence strolled past them.

"We have been left several times to fend for ourselves and the authorities tell media we are taking care of. At times, we lack, water, and shelter. Some of us stay in the forest for years fighting to keep the country from the rebels. Some die in the forest with their names and they are never remembered." He quoted Ola. Aisha's mind flashed back to what Sergeant Keshi told her when they were heading for the camp. Rebecca was keen to listen as baba continued.

"We were ambushed at Damsak. Many soldiers lost their lives. We didn't know what was before us. Some of us escaped but twenty died while defending their country. After that say many of us became less motivated to fight the rebels as we only get false promises and masked hopes. Many of us that survived began to wonder if there is an informant among us. How did the rebels know we are passing through a particular path? Many thoughts passed through our minds, but who are we to express our grievances that won't be attended to? He quoted Haruna. "What about them? Rebecca asked.

"Before they left to reclaim Damsak, their last words still ring in my heart. They knew they would die. They knew it would worth it if they die while protecting the country from the rebels. The screams of gunshots and IED explosions have affected Ola's eardrums and Haruna had an injury on his head."

'If I die, tell my wife and children not to cry. Tell my parents and siblings to remain strong. Death is not the end of life. If we don't give our lives for the country, who will? I will fall a hero, yes, a hero even if I am not celebrated." Haruna said and wiped his eyes. 'What we are fighting is deadlier than fear. We have sold out fears and death to the grave. I know I will fall but I won't fall a coward but a hero. Death is a necessary end." Ola said and shook his head." I was silently looking at them. I wanted to cry but I didn't. Haruna was fair, tall, and huge. A young Fulani man with a charming smile. He does not believe in failure but takes everything as the wish of Allah. He is married with two children. Ola is dark and of average height, with a fine voice. He is not married but has two children from different mothers. He believes God knows his end and anything that happens he will take it as his fate. Both of them died at the war front while fighting to protect the country. The soldiers reclaimed the local government but many lost their lives in the battle. There was an atmosphere of emotion, Aisha and Rebecca were wiping their teary eyes as baba sat mute and sighed heavily.

"The media tells you the soldiers are fine and they are taking care of. They cook up stories for us to believe. We fall for their truthful lies and believe the rebels have been defeated. We become confused and start doubting them because we don't know what else to believe." Rebecca said.

"We can't win terrorism in a day. What the soldiers are fighting against is strange. A group of people hiding behind the scenes to wreak havoc on the country. People who have sold their souls and have vowed to destroy everyone who goes against them." Aisha said as she wiped the remaining tears in her eyes.

At times, you wonder how the soldiers at the front line survive. How they go throughout a day fighting some sects that have decided to disturb the country over what is haram and not? How they come face to face with death while protecting their country. What we hear from the media about the soldier are different from what they face in the bush. How do you expect a man who had fled death, faced a different ambush, to treat you after the survival. We stay far, call them all sorts of names, bastards, fools, mumu, etc, but we fail to see their sacrifices. How many of them become impoverished and how they left their souls on the war front with death written all one them. They too have families, they want to live big. But for their country, many of them give their all.

"Sometimes when we try to run from our conscience, we come to discover that we look exactly like the lies and fears we tell ourselves. may Allah keep us safe," Baba said and picked up his radio while the young girls bade him goodnight and left for their tents.

Chapter 10

Scary pains of silence

My name is Hannatu I am from Chibok. I am 16 years old. My parents and siblings were murdered by the rebels on their farm. I was lucky to escape from the village before they attacked. When the gunmen arrived in my home town late at night in a blaze of gunfire chatting in an unfamiliar language.

Some of the villagers managed to escape, some were burnt alive while some were beheaded. Those that escaped ran through different directions mostly by jumping by running off into the bushes and the forest of no return. They ran along with their fears without looking back on what or who they left behind. The rebels took along with them the soul of the village with some of our girls whom they kidnapped from their school.

I would have been among them but I feel sick that day and decided to stay back at home and take care of myself. The cloud was frowning that day all we were hearing from a distance was gunshots, we all ran for our lives of lying to return after the frowns had given way to a raped village. Two of my friends and a cousin of mine were kidnapped. When I heard it, I was filled with scary pains of silence. Every day brought its fear. Fear of death, of being kidnapped, of oneself, of running away from home, of the rebels... Many fear that I was not able to recollect.

I was brought to the camp along with some people. We looked dejected, sorrowful, and filled with hatred for the rebels for making us flee from our homes. Many schools in my village were shut down. The rebels were against us going to school because they were believed education is evil and it contradicts and corrupts their unclear values and belief. Our schools were burnt down and used as their hideout and also for animals looking for a habit.

The first day I got to the camp, I met many faces with different painful emotions painted on their grieving faces. I felt like the camp might have been terrible for them. Complaints enveloped the sky and children wailed loudly trying to grip their sick mothers' breasts to suck out the remaining hope they are trying to lean on. My coming into the camp brought me face to face another phase of hardship, sorrow, pains, death, and uttermost rejection. Dreams were lying down in pain and embracing death day by day. Life to us became a mixture of joy and sorrow. For the past two days, we were left to starve while we awaited scanty supplies. We were not allowed to leave the camp in search of what to do for the fear of not returning to our ghosts. Most times we have to beg the camp heads to plead with the guards before they will give you the pass to go out not far from the camp under cruel conditions.

Some took advantage of our weaknesses to rape, force us into unsettled marriages, date, or do whatsoever they like with us. We became their sex objects and anytime they do anything with us and give us some money, we are forced to keep the secrets and take them to our graves. We had to survive. We just had to. Some of us had no option than to surrender our bodies and soul to them. What is life when you are putting on another person's body and yours is nowhere to be found?

We only had one another to share our pains and how we feel about the way we are being treated in the camp. Since people hardly come to share in our pains and make us feel we are still loved, accepted, and cherished. At times, you are afraid to share your burdens and plans because you don't who to trust with your secrets. You are afraid because people change and they may reveal your secrets and use that to mock you behind you. I had been passing through emotional trauma and depression because I was raped by one of the camp officials who told me not to tell anyone and if I do he would deny me and make sure I suffer in the camp.

I had lived with that fear and was afraid to tell anyone. I didn't want to share the pains for the fear of death. What fear is worst than emotional fear? What fear I worst than seeing yourself dying slowly but you are too afraid to get hold of yourself? What type of fear is horrible than that of a death you see but is yet to come to you? Every dear is fear, but there are classes of fear. I came to know I was pregnant when I went to a rough-looking thatched clinic in the IDP camp for a check-up and nurse Fatima told me I was three months pregnant. I wept bitterly and cursed the crap official in my heart. Nurse Fatima was kind and lovely, she encouraged me and promised to take good care of me until I deliver the child. When I told the camp official he neglected me and said just should abort the child that he is not sure he owns the child. He told me he is married and can't allow anything to destroy his marriage. I felt helpless and thought of killing myself. Not until I met Aisha...

Chapter 11

GARBA (A soldier that refused to die)

My name is Garba. I am from Katsina State. I am a soldier who had lived many lives that were not mine. I had faced many ambushes, fought many battles, and escaped death. There are many things I do that I am afraid of but I just had to do them. Since I was sent to the battlefront, I had always come face to face with death with the hope that I will leave to tell the story of the horrors, pains, and silence that embraced my heart and that of my battalion when we came face to face with the rebels.

We fight every day with anticipation for the war to end but within we are left with mental struggles as we come to terms with our fates peeling our shadows little by little as we get closer to our calling graves. I remember when we were ambushed by the rebels in one village. It was a bloodbath, I was lucky to escape with Isa, Gobedenisa, John, Chima, and Tunde. Others were killed and some were taken, hostage. That day I thought I had gone. I thought I won't see my beautiful wife Zainab and my beautiful children Maimuna and Ashiru. I thought that was how I would be forgotten in the forest and given as a sacrificial lamb to vultures and wild animals along with my colleagues that bowed to death.

When we got to the barrack panting like people who had no words of their own. Our overall head was not happy that we didn't fight to the last. He tagged us cowards and said we will join another battalion to repel the rebels' attack in another village. We embarked on the village at 9 pm and it was raining cats and rats. We had no option than to jump into the trucks waiting patiently for us. We rested assured that since we didn't die in the ambush death was afraid of us. We held one another's hand and promised to be our brother's keeper. No one must betray the other to the rebels.

"Chima," I called him. He looked a little bit tired and famished. He is a tall handsome fair young man from the eastern part of Nigeria. He is muscular, brave, intelligent, and has a pointed nose with an Igbo accent that makes everyone wants to listen to him when he is talking. His wife had called him earlier from the east before we left that she was sick and was admitted to the hospital.

"Yes, Garba, you called me. Mainene?"He said.

"Aboki, I hope you are all right?" I said just to cheer him up.

"I am all right. I will be fine. I just need rest." He puts his head down.

Chima is the closest friend I have in the army.

He had saved me in many battles. He looks beyond our religious, ethnic, and tribal differences. One day, he told me that I was more than a brother to him and he will always stand by me. Likewise, Tunde, Isa, Gobedenisa, and John had been amazing colleagues. We vowed not to allow anything to make us betray one another. We fought the rebels together and did almost everything together. When we got to the camp we are supposed to lodge before going to attack the rebels. The sky had stopped weeping. The place looked like a ghost town. Empty classrooms with naked ceilings and rough writing on the walls 'death zone, haram, I will fuck all una mama and sisters, we must kill all the kafir, army na banza, thunder fire una federal government, death to all.' Fear gripped me but I came back to myself. A soldier must not show his fears, he should be stronger and fearless to face death. I brought out a picture with my wife and children smiling. I kissed the picture and kept it back in my front pocket. I felt a bit relieved and wore a smile that drowned my doubts.

At times, you wonder how soldiers in the front time survive. How we go throughout a day fighting some sects that have decided to disturb the country over what is Haram and not. How they come face to face with death, protecting the country that does not care about them. Some put on tattered uniforms, pairs of slippers into the battleground. What you hear in the media about the soldiers in the northeast another version of what we suffer in the forest trying to repel the rebels' various attacks. How do you expect a soldier who had fled death, faced a different ambush, and endured hunger to treat after the war?

Our commander called a few minutes when we got to the weeping camp to tell us we won't be attacking the rebels again. He said, the rebels had known we are around and they had retreated. Some of us were happy while some were not. The next day our supplies came late, many of us looked tired and famished but what would we have done if not to be patient. We know where we are hurt. We only had to encourage one another. We breastfed our doubts and hopes in silence and carried loads of depression in our hearts. The night was too eager to come, some of us retreated to sleep while some were watching over the place. No sooner we realized it than the rebels attacked our camp. We knew we had been sold out by a Judas among us or within. They came in troops and were shooting to deafen the night.

I woke up like one whose house was on fire and saw Chima trying to put on his booths and khaki. He was battle-ready to face death again. Others had positioned themselves. The rebels were shooting endlessly while we were planning to fiercely attack them. Before we could position ourselves they had surrounded us. Their guns were out of this world. Isa, Tunde, and John were shot dead in the gun battle, while Gobedenisa was nowhere to be found. I was all alone to face my fears. All alone to carry my cross. I was shooting like my life depended on every shot. I saw many dead soldiers on the ground even our commander was shot dead. Some soldiers were still battling with the rebels that realized they had run out of bullets and ran away into thin air. Everywhere became calm again only groanings of our casualties filled the air.

I was searching for Chima, I had seen the bodies of others and could not hold myself. We returned to the camp defiled by blood to gather the bodies of our colleagues that bowed to death. I looked closely at a barren tree beside the horrible camp and saw Chima sitting down with his head bowed. I went to him with gladness only to discover he was hit by a bullet. I shook him, "Aboki, wake up. You can't die." I said as my voice was trembling.

I could not hold my tears. I screamed to the top of my voice and carried him on my shoulder to the front of the camp where other soldiers were busy mourning their friends and treating their wounds...

Morning came with another face of sorrow and grief. We were to leave for the barrack to bury our fallen colleagues. I saw under my box a letter written by Chima to me. I opened it and was eager to read. I was moved to tears as I read it.

Dear Garba,

Aboki, I am afraid I won't make it alive to the barrack. You know somedays there won't be a song in one's heart but darkness and death all over one. I am glad I met you and you have assisted me in many ways.

 You were like a brother and friend to me. I hope you keep the spirit alive. Also, travel to the east and tell my wife not to weep for me. I died protecting my country from dark souls that want to destroy her peace. I died a hero and not a coward. Even if I didn't fell, I am proud I kept the faith. I am alive even in death. Tell her I love her and Chimere my son and I will always do.

Until we meet again my lovely friend. Stay strong. Stay unbowed. Refuse to die.

Yours,

Chima.

I fell on the floor trying to squeeze the remaining tears in my eyes. My life appeared to me in black and white like the image of silence. All my friends had died and I was left alone to embrace myself. Left alone in the forest of deception. Left alone in the ambush of deceit. Left alone to nurse my heart pierced with bullets of pain.

I asked myself if it were a crime to defend my country? If it were a crime to give up before the war would end? The life of every man is often its novel, sometimes a tragic one. I stood up and joined others to load the dead soldiers at the back of a truck waiting to take us to the barrack.

Chapter 11

Ralia

What if you are among us? What if you lost everything to violence and insurgency? What if you have nothing to hold unto but fear? What if you are the one in the IDP camp? What if?

I am worried about the future of my children. Before we came here we were doing well. They were in school and always happy. Their father was killed by the rebels since he died I had never been myself again. My children are still living in the trauma of what happened the night we left home.

I need help. I don't think I will live to see another day. I had been having a series of nightmares and all I do is neglect them. How do I help myself in this situation? I do not have the power of my own.

I have been constantly living in fear. Fear of being attacked and fear of returning to a home we had divorced. I don't sleep at night for fear of the unknown.

My son is sick and my daughter had been finding it difficult to trace the worries in my mind. I just want a better life for them.

I can't call this life. Even when the NGOs come to teach us some skills my mind is far away. I just don't like my life. I will leave every day like my last and weave memories in my heart. Abdullahi is sick and there is no medication for him. He only takes paracetamol Baba bought for me and the malnourished food we eat. I pray he survives because every day he gets worst... I just pray he survives.

Chapter 12

Mama Jamil

(There are tears hidden in a corner of our hearts)

I got married at the age of 18 to a lovely man who was a confidante, friend, and husband. My late husband and I used to have many properties in our home town. We were living happily with our children until the rebels came. My husband was killed along with his friend on a business trip while my son was hit by a stray bullet when the soldiers were fighting with the rebels somewhere in Dapachi.

ou know it is difficult. It is difficult to say yes to life. One can't escape one's fate. I have learned to sieve my fears. I know I can't do away with them totally, but as a widow and the worst without children you know how it feels to wake up alone with the grief of your loved ones that were killed and you had to escape from your home for the fear of being killed.

I was brought to the IDP camp along with my friend and her children. We had a long night in the bush running away from death before some soldiers rescued us from the shadows chasing after us. It was a sign of relief for us and that moment felt like heaven was closer to us. Every day in this camp is filled with mixed feelings of pain and joy. The condition we found ourselves are unbearable though we had no choice but to embrace our fates.

What will one who had no home do? What will one who is chased by death do? Our lives were nowhere to be found, only our naked silence was left with us. Many of us in this faceless camp is from Gwoza, Monguno, Marte, Guzamala, and Nganzai. We have no choice here other than to eat what we are given and do how we are instructed.

There are tears hidden in a corner of our hearts. Tears we can't disclose. Tears only we can understand. I am not living again even if I am alive. I have no family again.

What is life When you are alone in a world filled with yourself? My life is filled with traces of death. I may die one day, of depression, grief, sorrow, and untamed silence. I miss my family, my friend, my home, and the goodbyes and warm hugs of love. I am living in the shadow of conflict. I miss everything home used to be. I feel like a prisoner here.

Chapter 13

BABA

My name is Baba Salifu. I am from Borno state.

I lost my family in one of the Boko Haram attacks. I traveled to a nearby town in search of greener pastures only to return to a home I couldn't identify.

I wept until my heart couldn't bear it again and buried them in a shallow grave. I had no choice but to go to the IDP camp to stay. Life had not been fair to me since I lost my family, at the IDP camp I always see death, hunger, starvation, depression, and poverty pass through me and smile.

...

You blame the past and new government rather than tell yourself the truth and give your best to the country. You reign curses on the government but drown the hopes and aspirations of this country with tribal, religious, and ethnic sentiments. The agitation for freedom had been stopped several times because when you rise to fight for your right and hold the government accountable to free you from the shackles they are holding you with.

You are tagged unpatriotic and a terrorist, who wants to divide the interest of few greedy ones sponsoring terrorism in the country. You are judged by your religion and tribe. You are attacked with all the weapons they have as they try to stab your dreams, your hope, your vision, your future. Every day you wake up, you are faced with a thousand ways to die.

There are problems operation crocodile smile and python dance cannot stop. These problems have eaten deep into our system and are there to stay. This country is like a prostitute looking for foreign countries to spread her legs to while her people drown in the pool of loud silence occupied by poverty, terrorism, banditry, rituals, police brutality, and rivalry.

...

A country where you are kidnapped and the government stylishly mocks and blames you and at the same time smiles at you and leave you to die alone. A country where you see lies but circumstances beyond your control make you paint them as truth and wear them as makeups on your face.

You are forced to live a life that is not yours just to fit in, to abandon yourself for nothing. Every day you dream and pray to vote out the Pharaohs, but you come to realize you had been telling yourself lies and not being sincere with God in your prayers. This country can make you divorce yourself and force you to become depressed if you don't fight her.

In this country, praying, pleading, and struggling for better leadership is blasphemy. The more you want to believe we are one, the more you find reasons not to. You say this country will not kill you, before dawn, you are dead and she mourns you. James, my bosom friend died while believing in a better country. A country that slapped him several times on his hopeful face and pushed colossally blames on him. A country that pushed him to the wall and made him afraid of himself. His last word was "In this country, some of us die before our prayers are answered while some of us are filled with questions unanswered. Many of us will leave to see a new country. If we succeed, we succeed, if we die, we die, our children will continue. There is a story in everybody. "

This country has no respect for her people... She will tell you she will kill you and nothing will happen. She will judge you and want to stone you to death while she hides her sin. You cringe in apprehension and look at yourself only to see your fate showing you another version of yourself. When will this country be fine? This country is not cursed, if it is cursed we are all cursed, but this country is a hypocrite...

CHAPTER 14

IDP

they tell us to pose for a picture, we pose with smiles on our faces that are not our own only to discover that we are not the ones in charge of our various bodies. we had left them in the darkness of yesterday's dream. They tell us we will soon return home, but where is home? Is it the place that was attacked by the rebels or this camp that exposed our shame?

We sit on several pavements counting our breath and hoping we are still in the minds of those that promised to assist us. Those that parted us on the back and told us it will be well. Those that once visited and saw our plights told us they will get back to us. At times, we stop believing in people's promises because they have always shown us the other side of the doubt.

When you come out every day, you see faces and see death behind them. Those you count as one of your realities. You wonder why they are so much hopeful and half-dead even in the face of hardship and scarce care they seek. You can stay two days without having your bath during the dry seasons. You learn to live with diseases, trauma, depression, and untold rapes. You come to realize that there is no good in conflict and violence of any kind.

Since I came to this camp in 2009 with my mother and brother. I have always battled with one or two voices telling me I can't achieve my dreams of getting an education and fighting for the right of vulnerable women and sensitizing young girls to get an education.

 Many times, I felt left behind but I have always tried to adapt to my realities and tell fear to its face that I won't give in. That I won't be dragged to depression. That there is hope even in the storm there is a glimmer of hope...

Chapter 15

CHIBOK

On a black morning on April 14, 2014, when silence had enveloped the sky and the morning sun was not eager to shine on the heart of Chibok in far away Borno state. They came not one not two with sophisticated guns and scary black masks and four dusty vans, chanting in an unknown voice with a banner that reads 'Jama'atu Ahlis Sunna Lidda'awati Wal-Jihad', which in Arabic means "People Committed to the Propagation of the Prophet's Teachings and Jihad" to Chibok girls high school and took away some school girls who were seeking education to become their botties because a woman's place according to them is not getting the white man's education.

"Walahi, we will kill them all. They are now our wives and nobody can take them away from us. Western education is haram and if all the kafirs do not leave western education we will make sure the country has no peace and kill anyone that opposes us." one of the rebels bragged as he shoots in the air.

"We have taken them all captives, nothing and no one will stop us. Bastard unbelievers who have lost the way. We don't believe in Nigeria, we want our state. You all are bloody Kafirs. We will kill you all and take you, hostage, even the military can't stop us." another rebel bragged while others scream in unfamiliar voices in support.

"We will shot the doors of western education from them. No girl child in the North will ever go to school. A woman must not be educated. Allahu Akbar." they all chorused as if they had memorized it.

Some of the girls ran away not minding if they were shot, while others surrendered and were taking away far away from their homes, far away to be molested, asked to renounce their religion, and married out for a penny. The news gripped the country on her throat. Many questions were in the air, how did they gain access into the school? Why didn't the military men repel their attack? Who sold the girls to the rebels? These questions ran through many people's minds. How can a country fail to protect its citizens from attacks? What are they fighting against? You know a man's enemy is a member of his own house. Those selling us to them are with us.

The tradition of this country is full of religious differences, corruption, ethnic rivalries, and political instabilities. We are constantly fighting battles with faceless people young and old who have vowed to bury the country.

The country was in another state of mourning. Bring back our girl was on everyone's lip. Where are our girls? We can't tell. We only depended on the media to tell us different versions of their whereabout to calm our nerves. Many promises were in the air, "they will be found" "Our girls must return" "we will destroy the rebels and take the girls back." Unclear promises and questions mixed with the banality of dreams horrifying portraits and languished pains.

When matters of life and death we should confront comes, we leave them to God to solve, then also facing them with expectations. We call for prayer and fast, but go to sleep hoping we won't work again, we won't face our problems and look it in the face. How can our prayers be answered when we are not connected in the heart.

The Chibok girls' kidnap was not a rebellion against one but all. Against the girl child and her education. It is high time we asked ourselves some hard questions. Who are our enemies? What has happened to the rest girls? What about Leah Sharibu? Many years have gone and we are yet to find them. Will all our girls ever come back?

Chapter 16

AISHA

"Every child is just one caring adult away from being a success story." Josh Sipp."

my name is Aisha. I have come across many hurdles in life. I fled my home with my mother and brother because they came again to take away our remaining lives. It was a horrible journey for us, we followed through scary paths for fear of death. Fear of our home. Fear of being raped and taken hostage.

How does the death of a loved one come to you? For me, it came with a kind of pain that was too difficult to erase. You witness their deaths and see the whole world coming down in a day. In this camp, many bodies are disconnected from life but they are living with the hope that the sun will shine on them. My father was killed along with his friend. My mother died of high blood pressure in a morning that wore a sad look and Abdullahi my only brother died of sickness I don't know. Those moments were rough moments for me. I cried my eyes out as Baba and other grave diggers lowered their bodies into the already dug graves with scanty prayers on their lips as other camp dwellers wore sickly faces haunted by death.

I am an orphan now and I didn't bargain with death to bring me too much sorrow in a day. What is life, when you feel all alone in the world and those you feel will be with you will not always be there for you? At times, I wake up with strange voices that tell me I will die too.

 I will be killed by the rebels; I will be raped and molested by some evil camp officials as they did to other young girls. I keep thinking many things and fear of them all kept piling up in my heart. I see fear beside me laughing at me as I try to scold it to let me go. I fell depressed and mentally drained shaping my life around flashbacks and the present.

 At times, I try to shape my body with my condition and sleep in my tent with hunger in my head counting promises and the good days of life. I get stalked in silence, with nothing to say because my home had deserted me and I can't just imagine this as home, not in any way. Just last week, Adamu, Daniel, and Meshach fled from the camp, and until now we don't know where they went to.

"I am perturbed about my future and my life in this camp. I am not at peace with life here at times I smile but to keep hope alive. It is only God who knows when I will be free from the doubts I weave every day, from the tears I refuse to shade. I just need a better life I am unhappy with the one here.

 For how long will I continue to run away from myself? How long will I feel empty and drown in silence? There is much suicidal thought in my heart but I refuse to die. I can't take my life even if death is all around me telling me to give in. I know everything goodwill comes.

We are always assisted by a few NGOs and religious institutions that come to improve our lives and tell us to seek education and always stand for what is right. I don't know what the future holds for me, but I want to be educated.

I want to stand up for my right as first a human and secondly a woman. I want to tell other girls that they should seek education, improve themselves, skills, and nothing more.

With education, I will overcome the cage of ignorance and open my heart for self-discovery.

I know one day I will leave this camp and pursue my dreams but I have to keep sensitizing other camp dwellers about the importance of education that will free them from mental slavery. There is nothing good about ignorance. I have learned many things from the NGO's and they have exposed me to the true meaning of education. I have no fear again.

There is no true assurance that home will be free again, every day is occupied with good bad news, but against all odds, we shall overcome. I am happy here even if it looks like death is always haunting me here because anywhere that shades me is home.